Naomi's Gift

WRITTEN AND ILLUSTRATED BY
SCOTT FREEMAN

BIG PICTURE
PUBLISHING

Special thanks to: the Loveland Museum/Gallery; my lovely models, Rachel Dowd, Sarah Baker, and Sierra Freeman; Sandy Beegle and her harp; Trisha and Chase Swift; and Mollie for her enduring love.

Editors: Christy Fagerlin, Kristin Fenwick   Book design: Scott Freeman

Mail requests to: Permissions, Big Picture Publishing, 185 N Harrison Ave., Loveland, CO 80537

Signature Book Printing, *www.sbpbooks.com*, Printed in Hong Kong.

Library of Congress Catalog-in-Publication Data

Freeman, Scott
    Naomi's Gift/ by Scott Freeman; illustrations by Scott Freeman
        p.   cm.
    Summary: A small-town doctor struggles with his decision to deliver a
            disabled baby. One Christmas Eve a mysterious musician
            enables him to make peace with his decision.

    ISBN 1-932433-68-6

About This Story ...

Naomi's Gift is based on a true story. Practicing in the 1920s, Dr. Frederic Loomis really did reluctantly deliver a breech baby having Naomi's unusual deformity. Years later, in that same hospital, a trio of young ladies performed in the hospital Christmas program. Dr. Loomis was present at that program and was particularly captivated by the graceful harpist. Afterward, this young musician proved to be instrumental in helping the doctor make peace with his decision to bring a severely disabled baby into the world. You can read Dr. Loomis' original story, The Tiny Foot, in Joe Wheeler's Christmas in My Heart 2, Review and Herald Publishing, 1993.

Some may wonder why I adapted an already great story. Dr. Loomis' original story did not work as a children's storybook for several reasons. First, the entire story takes place within the walls of a hospital. In the story's new setting, readers can enjoy seeing snow, horses, and a small western town near the turn of the 20th century. More importantly, Dr. Loomis' telling of his story, though engaging for adults, is less friendly for children. For example, being a doctor, he talks at length about breech pregnancy and the birthing process. Finally, on a more personal note, for me a great Christmas story is not complete without some acknowledgement of the reason we have a great holiday called Christmas.

For those of you who know and love the original story, The Tiny Foot, I hope you will overlook my embellishments and enjoy this adaptation as true to the spirit of the original.

Scott Freeman

Naomi's Gift

WRITTEN AND ILLUSTRATED BY
SCOTT FREEMAN

BIG PICTURE
PUBLISHING

Special thanks to: the Loveland Museum/Gallery; my lovely models, Rachel Dowd, Sarah Baker, and Sierra Freeman; Sandy Beegle and her harp; Trisha and Chase Swift; and Mollie for her enduring love.

Editors: Christy Fagerlin, Kristin Fenwick   Book design: Scott Freeman

Mail requests to: Permissions, Big Picture Publishing, 185 N Harrison Ave., Loveland, CO 80537

Signature Book Printing, *www.sbpbooks.com*, Printed in Hong Kong.

Library of Congress Catalog-in-Publication Data

Freeman, Scott
    Naomi's Gift/ by Scott Freeman; illustrations by Scott Freeman
        p.   cm.
      Summary: A small-town doctor struggles with his decision to deliver a
           disabled baby. One Christmas Eve a mysterious musician
           enables him to make peace with his decision.

      ISBN 1-932433-68-6

About This Story ...

Naomi's Gift is based on a true story. Practicing in the 1920s, Dr. Frederic Loomis really did reluctantly deliver a breech baby having Naomi's unusual deformity. Years later, in that same hospital, a trio of young ladies performed in the hospital Christmas program. Dr. Loomis was present at that program and was particularly captivated by the graceful harpist. Afterward, this young musician proved to be instrumental in helping the doctor make peace with his decision to bring a severely disabled baby into the world. You can read Dr. Loomis' original story, The Tiny Foot, in Joe Wheeler's Christmas in My Heart 2, Review and Herald Publishing, 1993.

Some may wonder why I adapted an already great story. Dr. Loomis' original story did not work as a children's storybook for several reasons. First, the entire story takes place within the walls of a hospital. In the story's new setting, readers can enjoy seeing snow, horses, and a small western town near the turn of the 20th century. More importantly, Dr. Loomis' telling of his story, though engaging for adults, is less friendly for children. For example, being a doctor, he talks at length about breech pregnancy and the birthing process. Finally, on a more personal note, for me a great Christmas story is not complete without some acknowledgement of the reason we have a great holiday called Christmas.

For those of you who know and love the original story, The Tiny Foot, I hope you will overlook my embellishments and enjoy this adaptation as true to the spirit of the original.

Scott Freeman

Naomi's Gift

SCOTT FREEMAN

Loosely adapted from Dr. Frederic Loomis' timeless true story,
The Tiny Foot

◆

In memory of Mom,
whose childlike heart brightened all of my Christmases.

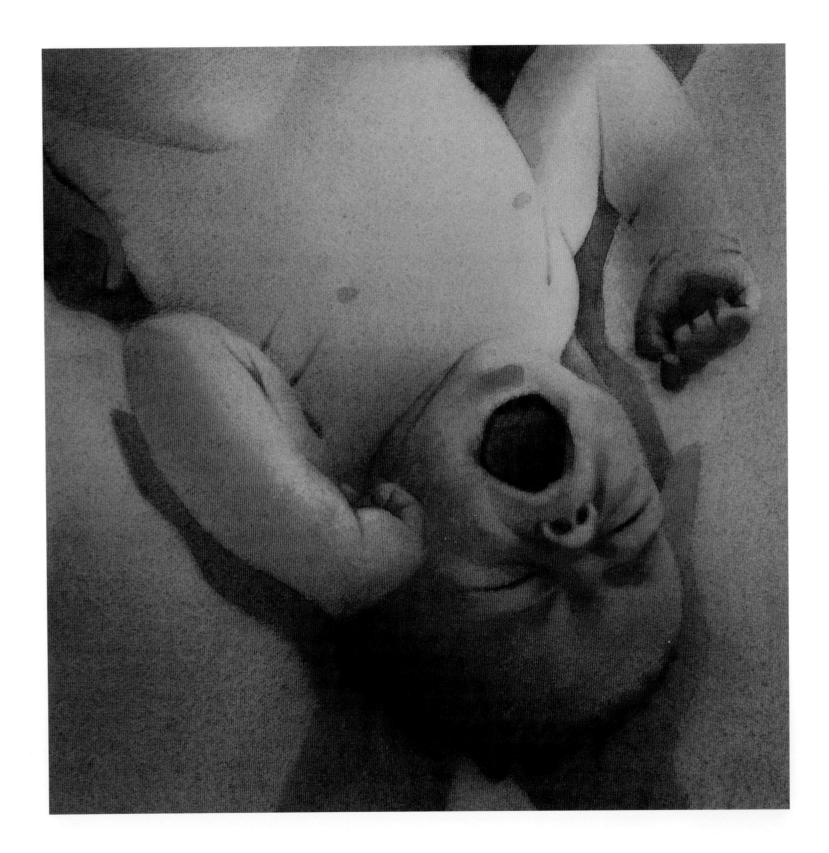

It was the day before Christmas, a day I would remember for the rest of my life. I was the only doctor in town, and I was on my way to deliver my second baby in a single day. The first delivery had been a very special one for me. I've had many good days in my life, but this morning was one of the happiest, for I had the indescribable joy of delivering my firstborn — a son. He was a perfect, curly-headed, barrel-chested little rascal, hollering for all he was worth. I was beside myself with joy. I couldn't take my eyes off my wife, Gretta, and our new baby boy. I wanted to stay with them forever, but it was only three hours later when I received word that the Hosea's baby was on the way.

I married late in life, and God had blessed me with a very patient and understanding wife. It seemed our life together was constantly interrupted, but Gretta never said a word. She knew I hated leaving now more than ever, but duty was calling again. I kissed her and our new son at her breast. I breathed in their warm scent one last time, grabbed my black bag and my coat, and hurried outside into the cold, grey afternoon.

I knew the Hosea's place well as Mrs. Hosea was frequently ill. It was more than a mile out of town. The Hoseas were a respectable couple — poor farmers, barely scraping by, but they were good, honest people. I wondered if God might give them a son, too, to help with the farm and maybe take it over someday. I rode hard, hoping I wouldn't be too late. I needn't have worried. It would be a long, hard labor. It would also turn out to be the most difficult delivery I would ever perform.

Upon examining the mother, I found the baby in a breech position. This meant that the baby would enter the world feet, or bottom first, rather than head first, in the usual way. This sobered me. The death rate for breech babies is comparatively high because once the body is born, the head remains inside of the mother to be delivered. At that point, the umbilical cord becomes compressed between the baby's head and the mother's pelvis, cutting off oxygen to the baby. If the head is not delivered soon thereafter, the baby will die within a few short minutes.

When the time for the delivery had finally come, I gently drew down one little foot. I took hold of the other one, but for some reason I could not understand, it would not come down beside the first one. With the next contraction, the baby's body emerged enough that I could see that it was a little girl. Only then did I see that the second foot would never be beside the first one. The entire lower leg was missing, with the second foot attached where the knee should have been. So a baby girl was to suffer this strange defect, the likes of which I had never before seen, nor have I since.

As I waited for the next contraction, a string of thoughts came to me, and with them, a terrible dilemma. I thought of how the Hoseas might react to this circumstance. I knew the character of this family. I felt certain that they would further impoverish themselves trying everything they could with every famous orthopedist who might offer them a ray of hope. Most of all, I thought of this little girl sitting sadly by herself while other girls laughed and danced and ran and played. And then I realized it was in my power to spare this family and this little girl a lifetime of suffering.

It is not uncommon for breech babies to die in delivery if the delivery is too slow. If I were to delay *this* delivery — to wait just a minute too long — then this baby would never take her first breath of air. This family would be spared a world of grief. It would not be an easy delivery anyway. The Hoseas, after the initial shock of loss, would probably not regret losing a child so sadly handicapped. In a year or so they would try again, and this tragic occurrence would never be repeated.

So I held this baby's very life in my hands, and the clock was ticking. No one suspected what I was thinking. As a doctor of medicine, I had never before

entertained such a thought as this, but as I glanced down at the pitiful foot in my hand, a pang of sorrow for the baby's future swept through me. I made up my mind that the merciful course would be for me to perform an "unsuccessful delivery."

The next contraction began. If I could delay just two or three more minutes, then all of this would be over. I delivered the shoulders, knowing that the cord was now hopelessly compressed. I struggled mightily with my conscience. Was this really my decision to make?

As if in answer to that unspoken question, the baby suddenly began to struggle. I felt a strong surge of life as she kicked forcefully in my hand with her good leg. This was too much for me. I could not go through with my plan. I quickly delivered a malformed, but otherwise healthy, baby girl. The Hoseas were overjoyed. They scarcely seemed to notice her deformity. After a time, as mother and baby seemed to be doing well, I left some instructions with Mr. Hosea. Congratulating them and promising to return the next day, I headed back home. I remember I could not bring myself to say "Merry Christmas" to the Hoseas that night. It seemed too ironic a thing to say, knowing the broken gift I was leaving with them.

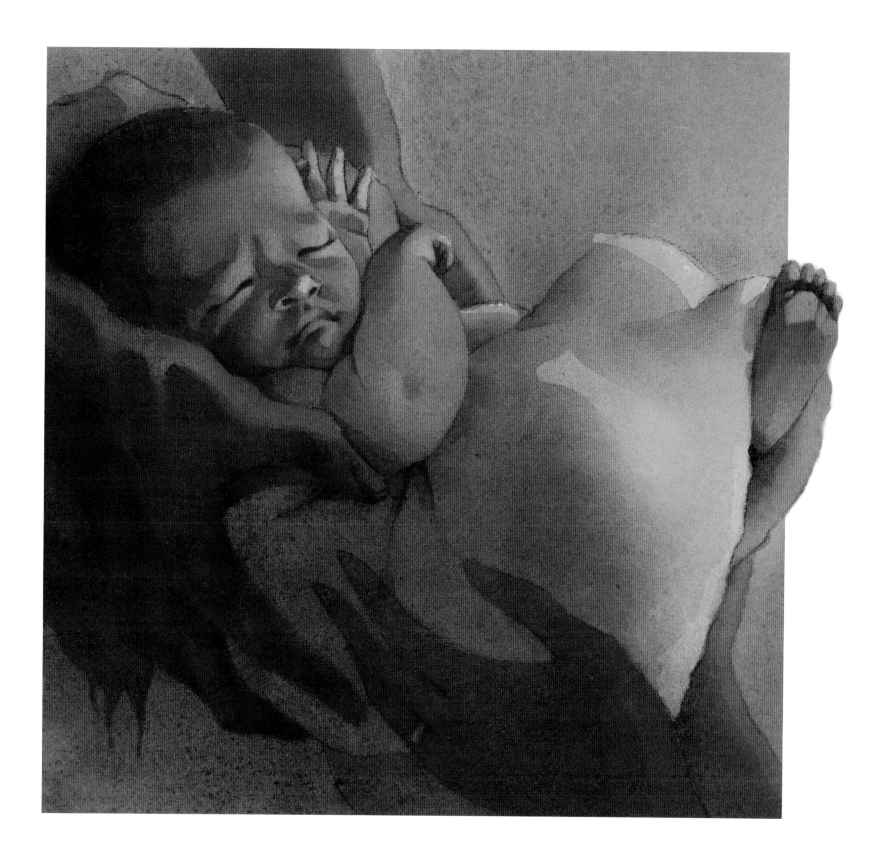

I remember being frustrated with God on the way home that cold night. "Why must these things happen?" I shouted upward, into the falling snow. "Did not your only begotten say that if we ask you for bread, you will not give us a stone? ... And if this had to happen, couldn't you have at least made me strong enough to spare this family from this tragedy?"

I had gone from the pinnacle of joy that morning, to the depths of despair and uncertainty that night. I was utterly exhausted. I arrived at home in the wee hours of Christmas morning to find my Gretta and our new son sleeping together peacefully. Slowly, joy overshadowed my troubled emotions, and I drifted off to sleep.

In the months that followed, all of my fears for the Hoseas came true. Mr. Hosea worked himself thin trying to bring in extra income. Within a year's time they sold the farm they loved and moved away, seeking treatment for their little girl. I would hear reports of them from time to time. They had been to specialists in St. Louis. Then Chicago. Eventually I lost track of them completely. I blamed myself bitterly for not having had the strength to yield to my temptation.

Gretta and I had two more children, both boys. Our little family grew, along with our little town, all of which kept me busier than ever. Gretta remained ever patient and forbearing, despite having three boys to raise. They were more than a handful. There were many times I was glad to be a doctor while raising those boys. But never was I more grateful for my profession than on one remarkable Christmas Eve.

There was to be a special Christmas Eve service at the church that night. Our two younger boys were singing in the program. Our oldest, who had been away at college back East, was coming home. Furthermore, he was to bring his new fiancé home to meet us. I was filled with anticipation, but predictably, I was kept busy making calls all day and into the evening. My last call was to a homebound elderly woman, the widow McCullough. She did have a bad cold, but what she really needed was company. She made it clear to me several times that she wanted to be at the church, but I would not let her go out. I visited with her for quite a while though, and by the time I got to the church, I had missed half the program. The church was filled to overflowing. There were even a few horseless carriages parked outside with the horses and wagons. I knew one of these belonged to my son.

Folks were accustomed to seeing the Doc sneak in late to church. As was her habit, Gretta had saved a seat for me near the front, so I stole my way to her side during a round of applause. I kissed her glowing face, and she smiled at me and took my hand. On the stage, three lovely young ladies in white gowns — a violinist, a cellist, and a harpist — were just seating themselves. I have always loved the harp, and I was thrilled to not have missed this part of the service. As they began to play, I was mesmerized. The harpist played flawlessly, with remarkable grace and worshipful beauty. They were playing a new Christmas carol, *In the Bleak Midwinter.* The words went to my heart.

> *In the bleak midwinter, frosty wind made moan,*
> *Earth stood hard as iron, water like a stone;*
> *Snow had fallen, snow on snow,*
> *Snow on snow,*
> *In the bleak midwinter, long ago*

My mind shot back, as it often did on Christmas Eve, to that troubled night, long ago when I delivered a deformed child into the world. The dark and now familiar feelings of uncertainty clouded my spirit again.

Then began the strains of another carol, and the harpist began to sing. She sang as beautifully as she played. Her countenance was as beautiful as her singing. Inexplicably, the cloud over my spirit began to lift as she sang.

O holy night, the stars are brightly shining; it is the night of our dear Savior's birth
Long lay the world in sin and error pining, 'til He appeared and the soul felt its worth
A thrill of hope, the weary world rejoices, for yonder breaks a new and glorious morn

As when the shepherd boy David played his harp before King Saul, so now, my darkness was being driven away. In its place were the perfect peace of God and a fresh sense of His sovereignty regarding all that had happened on that troubled night those years ago. Silently, I thanked Him for this minister of His grace.

When the service was over, I only wanted a word with the harpist. I climbed onto the stage to meet her. She stood still, listening, with one hand on her harp as I tried to explain to her how God had touched my heart as she sang. Suddenly, my son appeared at my side, greeting me with an embrace.

"I see you've met my fiancé," he smiled, his eyes sparkling. I looked at him. Then at her.

"*This* is your fiancé?" I asked, incredulous. "Are you sure you deserve such a treasure?" I asked.

"I'm sure I do not," he said gazing at her. "Pa, may I have the pleasure of introducing you to your future daughter-in-law, Miss Naomi Hosea."

At these words, my mouth fell open. As she stepped forward to offer her hand, I noticed for the first time, a slight limp. All at once the truth washed over me. "Do you know who this is!" I cried to my son. Their beaming faces told me that they both knew that she was the poor baby I had delivered on Christmas Eve those years ago. But only God knew of my inner struggle that night and of the terrible deed I had almost committed. "Dear God, thank you," I managed to say, and then, I could no longer speak. Tears filled my eyes as I took this precious jewel into my arms and held her.

"It was all I could do to convince Naomi's mother to let her come here for the holidays," my son explained. "She's their pride and joy. But the Hoseas wanted you to see the young lady that the baby you delivered has become."

That concert made me the most grateful doctor in all the world. It was said afterward that an angel sang in our church that night. I know better than anyone that it was not an angel, but flesh and blood. It was flesh and blood marred by the fall, but made fearfully and wonderfully glorious by the grace and the Spirit of God. That grace was revealed in the likeness of human flesh centuries ago, on the very first Christmas Eve. Angels really did appear on that night above all nights. Above the Judean foothills, they heralded the arrival of God's Messiah; His final answer to the cries of broken humanity. In our day, His gift of grace continues to give life to all who will humbly receive it. So we, the broken, are reborn on the inside to await that day when He makes *all* things new.

While we wait, there are moments now and then, and especially at Christmastime, when the light of God breaks through the everyday brokenness. During those moments we see a faint glimmer of the bright joy that awaits us. The best one of those moments for me was the night Naomi played her harp in our little town.